I0692135

Also by Maris D'souza:

Sirena's Tears: A Story about Forgiveness from the Island of Guam

Sirena's Heart:

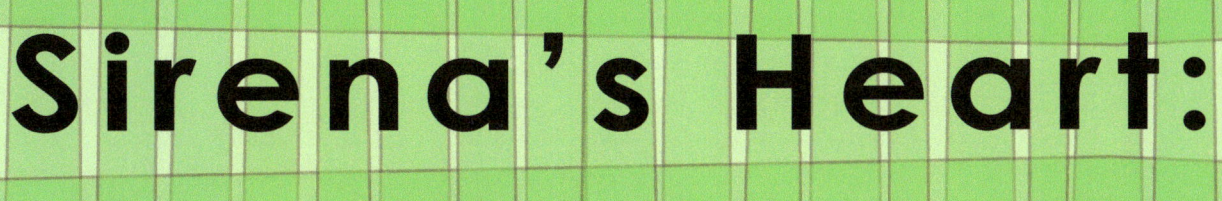

A Story about Love...Guam-Style!

Story and Illustrations by Maris D'souza

Copyright © 2010 by Maris D'souza. All rights reserved.

No part of this book may be reproduced, stored in a retrieval system, or transmitted, in part or in whole, without the express written permission of the author.

Scripture texts in this work are taken from the New American Bible, revised edition © 2010, 1991, 1986, 1970 Confraternity of Christian Doctrine, Washington, D.C. and are used by permission of the copyright owner. All Rights Reserved. No part of the New American Bible may be reproduced in any form without permission in writing from the copyright owner.

ISBN: 978-0-615-42688-4

Library of Congress Number: 2010918068

Book cover design and all artwork copyright © 2010 by Maris D'souza

Published by
RJD Consulting
P.O. Box 5288
Frisco, TX 75035

www.sirenatoday.moonfruit.com

Printed in the United States of America

This story is dedicated to the Sirena which lies within every human heart, searching for truth, happiness, and love.

Then Peter approaching asked him, "Lord, if my brother sins against me, how often must I forgive him? As many as seven times?" Jesus answered, "I say to you, not seven times but seventy-seven times.

(Matthew 18:21-22)

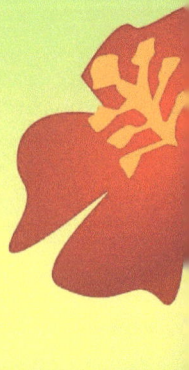

Once upon a time there was a young woman named Sirena Santos from the sunny island of Guam. Sirena was a wild child. She was wildly passionate. She was passionate about meeting people—mostly boys. She was passionate about dancing—with boys. She was passionate about singing out loud—to boys—and sauntering around the beach in her coconut shell bikini top and hula skirt.

She craved attention. This drove her mama crazy. "**Ai adai**, Sirena! **Oh my goodness**, what are you wearing? Cover yourself, girl! You have no respect! Where do you think you're going dressed like that? I need help with the laundry today!" her mama, Manuela Santos, cried out.

Sirena replied with her wicked tongue, "No way, lady. Do the laundry yourself. Like, whatever! I'm going to hit the beach."

She was living large, buying expensive clothing with her mama's money, talking on her fancy cell phone like she was a famous supermodel, and cruising around in her **Guam bomb**, a rusty, beat-up old pick-up truck.

Mama Manuela was upset with Sirena for being so **disatenta**, or **disrespectful**, but she really loved her. Sirena had it all. She was lucky. She was spoiled. She broke her mama's heart. Still, she wasn't happy. She wasn't satisfied. She felt empty and kept wanting more and more of something. It was like an ache in her heart and a longing to be loved without knowing what *love* really meant.

"What is this pain in my heart?" Sirena cried. "Maybe a new *seven-day bracelet* will make me feel better—and a new boyfriend, too!"

Mama Manuela was upset.

Sirena really didn't care.

But the more clothing she bought from the *Dededo Flea Market*, the emptier she felt. And the more boys she hung out with by the barbecue pit at the *Chamoru Village*, the worse she felt. It was fun for a while, but then it got old.

That's when things got bad. "Everybody say party!" Sirena yelled as she danced recklessly, night after night, at parties and techno clubs. For some reason, she thought that dancing all night would make her feel better. It kept her distracted, but mostly it just made her feel tired the next day.

Sirena shut her heart off to block the pain. "Life stinks. Nobody loves me," she muttered. She was frustrated, she was flunking out of her cosmetology class at Guam Community College, and making careless mistakes at her cashier job at the *Tamuning Muck-Donood*'s restaurant. She never felt too pretty either, no matter how much eyeliner she smeared around her eyeballs. People thought she was a sweet girl because she had a friendly smile, but she felt cruddy on the inside. Sirena wanted to run away from Guam very badly.

Let's show 'em we're "tuff"!

Dancing all night made Sirena feel tired the next day.

Inner beauty? What's that?

Self-centered? Who me?

Sirena had many distractions, but she still felt empty.

I need extra brown powa!

"I'm swimming away to the U.S. and leaving this island for good," Sirena declared one day. She was named after a beautiful legendary mermaid, so she thought swimming to America seemed perfectly smart. After jumping into the ocean, however, she suddenly realized something: she was a strong swimmer, but not *that* strong.

Sirena decided to take a flight to the U.S. instead. She demanded that Mama Manuela buy her a plane ticket so she could flee to Washington State and attend school there. Despite embarrassingly low S.A.T. scores, she had miraculously gained admission into a small technical college. Sirena was ready to pack her bags and escape to the West Coast, and she whined and begged until Mama Manuela caved in as usual, allowing her to take off abruptly to the states.

Sirena's departure brought great sadness to Mama Manuela's very soul. She had raised Sirena all by herself since her husband had died 18 years ago from liver disease when Sirena was just a baby. This made seeing her only daughter leave home almost unbearable, but she silently let her go.

Sirena hurriedly hugged Mama Manuela and told her goodbye before enthusiastically boarding the plane. She fantasized about her bright and sunny future in America as her heart leapt with excitement during the 24-hour excursion. When she landed in the U.S., however, she felt small and uncertain. The frosty winter wind chilled her to the bone, and she felt so bitterly cold inside. It was her dream to move far away, but boy was it different.

There was no Mama to hear her whine. There were so many **unknown American**, or *haolie* faces, and so many places to go for miles and miles. It was scary. It was exciting. It was confusing. Her life was changing so fast.

Just 5,000 more miles to go!

GUAM

U.S.A.

Sirena broke her mama's heart.

Sirena felt cold when she left Guam.

Sirena quickly started school, found a job, and settled into her dormitory with her new roommate, Brenda, from the Philippines. Things were great at her college. There was a huge flow of attention from boys, and she absolutely loved it. Only one boy captured her heart though. He was sincere, funny, and head-over-heels for her. His name was Andy. He wore a black leather jacket, had a funny little mustache, and a fascinating foreign accent.

Sirena and Andy were total opposites but totally attracted to each other. Andy enjoyed Sirena's fun and bubbly nature, while Sirena admired Andy's serious and macho persona. "Will you be my *gull-friend, Seeray-nuh*?" Andy asked with his thick Hungarian accent. "You mean *girlfriend*? Sure! Why not?" Sirena said as she giggled happily. Sirena and Andy spent all their time together. They went around town in his rickety red car, seeing all the sights. They took classes together, worked at the same burger joint, and had all the same friends.

Andy and Sirena instantly fell in love. "I know all your dreams in life will come true!" Sirena told Andy as they walked around their college campus. "I know yours will, too! I'll always be there for you. I love you, Seeray-nuh!" Andy told her as he held her hand tightly.

Andy was dedicated, caring, and always looked out for Sirena. He gallantly walked her to her dormitory every night, making sure that she was safely inside, and he always jumped to her aid when she needed help. Andy could be rather grouchy, impatient, and stubborn at times, but Sirena knew he had a heart of gold. She could see that Andy was someone who would walk a mile just to help a stranger carry a heavy load. The way that he eagerly served others reminded her of the love of Christ. He had a simple, quiet love for Jesus that touched Sirena's heart.

Sirena was fully devoted to Andy. She comforted and encouraged him every day. She created homemade cards and presents to show him her love. She cooked for him often, although she only knew how to make **chicken kelaguen** and **red rice,** her favorite **Guam dishes.** Andy could see that she put her heart into it, so that made him happy.

Sometimes they would argue though. "I don't understand you!" Sirena would cry. "You never listen to me!" Andy would yell back. They would break up on Monday and be back together by Tuesday. This went on for years. It was like a tug-of-war game. They drove each other a little crazy, but they were definitely crazy about each other.

Sirena and Andy fell in love.

When they finally graduated from college, they were still in love, but Andy ended up moving to North Dakota to start a new job. Andy and Sirena were thrust into a long-distance relationship, which tore Sirena up inside. She had started working in a busy insurance office, but she thought about Andy every day as she stared forlornly at her paperwork.

Life seemed so confusing. Sometimes she missed Andy terribly, and sometimes she felt so homesick for Guam. Andy and Sirena talked about marriage over the telephone, but it never seemed quite right. They argued frequently and had a hard time understanding each other's feelings. Sirena could barely even understand herself. "Where's my life going? Something's missing, but what is it?" Sirena moaned.

For five long years, Sirena worked at the insurance office, and time kept passing by as she pondered about life. At the age of 27, she felt all grown up and wanted to make a big change. "I'm tired of being in a dead-end relationship," she said. A few days after she had made that statement, Sirena and Andy officially dumped each other. Their long distance relationship had dragged on for way too many years. Sirena was devastated. Breaking up was much more painful than she had anticipated. "I'll never love again! I'm quitting my job and running home to Guam," she said as she sobbed uncontrollably.

Sirena hopped on a plane and moved back to Guam on a trial basis. She was so happy to be home—for about a minute. The trade winds caressed her heart, the sunsets pierced her soul, and Mama Manuela's commanding voice reverberated through her eardrums. Within a few months of living at home, Sirena felt like she was suffocating and wanted to return to America. She missed Andy like crazy and hoped someday they would reunite and get married. She also dreamed of an exciting career.

Once again, she hopped on a plane and headed for Washington State. "I just need an interesting job! I'll work for a big, huge company and that will erase this pain in my heart," she said cheerfully. She was thrilled when she was hired immediately as an executive assistant for a prestigious public relations firm. Her new job kept her mind occupied for a little while, but then she got bored, and yet another year passed.

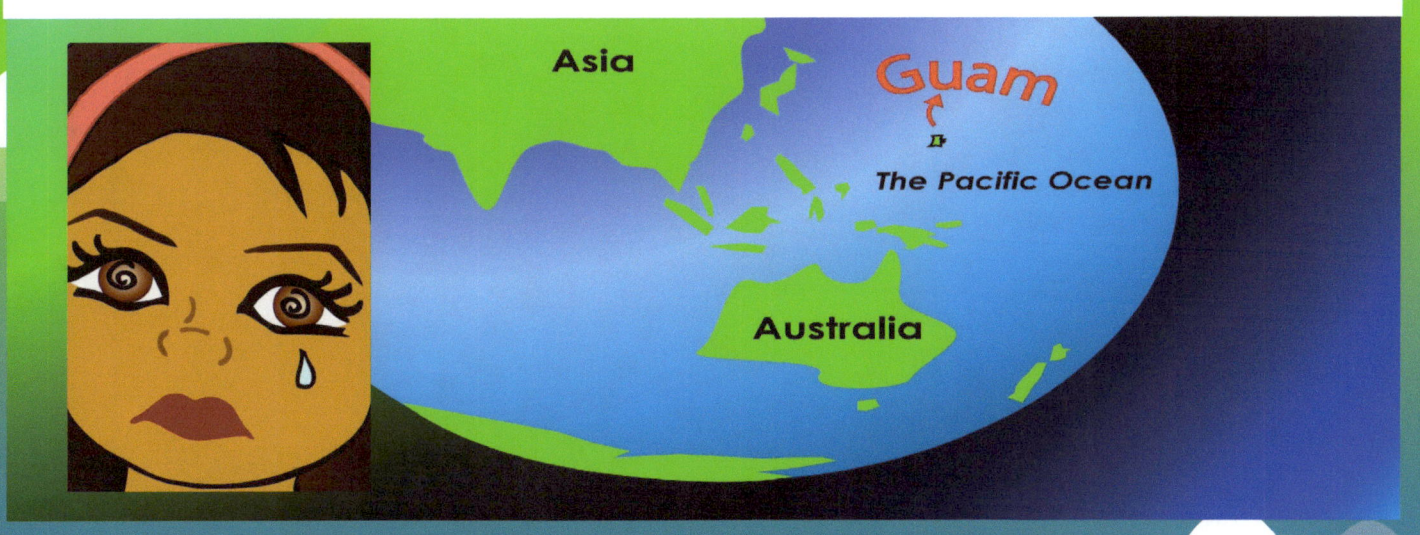

During that year, Andy thought about Sirena often. He still lived in North Dakota, but he called Sirena on the phone, hoping they could get back together. Sadly, their conversation ended in tears. "I want to be with you, Andy, but you don't love me enough. How can we be together when we never talk about our problems? We never even hear each other out. Can you promise things will be different this time? Let's just forget about each other!" Sirena cried mournfully. She wished Andy would reassure her that everything was going to be all right. She wished he would show just a little bit of understanding. It was so frustrating explaining this to him. It felt like pure torture.

"Why are you complaining, Seeray-nuh? I made a big mistake calling you. We never had any problems! You give me a headache. That's the only problem I have. I don't have time for this! Who do you think you are, anyway? " Andy shouted, wishing that Sirena could just trust him and listen to him. It made him feel so terrible when she complained. *Why couldn't things go smoothly between them?*

"You're no prize either, Andy! Don't call me anymore! It's over between us!" Sirena snapped back. "I won't ever call you again, Seeray-nuh! Good luck and goodbye!" Andy yelled as his temper flared and his pride took over. And then CLICK! Out of fear and disgust, they hung up on each other.

"Maybe I am a loser. Maybe I am just a nothing and a nobody," Sirena said with a sigh. She wished she could be at peace with Andy, but she had no idea how they could make that happen. The only thing Sirena believed she could do was just give up and walk away in misery. Her head was filled with doubt and discouragement, thinking that nothing in life was possible and that no one really loved her. Sirena hopelessly gave in to these thoughts every time.

The next day, Sirena indulged in a shopping spree to cheer herself up. She bought the tightest *Harm-ani* jeans and the tiniest tube top in the store. She then strutted around in her thickest pair of **zories,** which were her favorite **slippers**, but she still felt gloomy. "I want to go out. I wish I had a date," she declared.

Andy called Sirena on the telephone.

Sirena cried and cried.

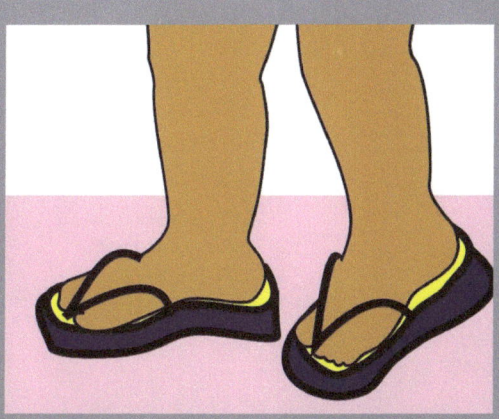

Shopping Addiction!

Wearing extra-thick zories
(slippers) did not bring Sirena any comfort.

Sirena hit the internet and went straight to her *My Spaced-Out Page*. She had plenty of admirers and about three million internet friends. After a few flirtatious e-mail messages and a dozen phone calls, she found herself a dinner date.

At dinner, Sirena chewed on her fake French manicure. "Ugh, and I thought I was selfish," she mumbled as her date bragged endlessly about himself. She then went straight home to search online for another date.

At dinner with the next dude, she pulled at her hair extensions as her date droned on about his personal problems. "Gosh, and I thought I was depressed. I am so out of here," she said to herself. As soon as she finished yawning a few times out of boredom, she grabbed her purse and left.

Sirena yawned as her date discussed his personal problems.

Sirena had plenty of so-called friends.

Sirena's mood swings really weren't cute at all.

That night, Sirena ran back to her apartment in despair. She felt so alone. She felt lost. She wanted to blame the whole world for her miserable life. For several months after that, she constantly complained to her outspoken Filipina friend and former college roommate, Brenda, about how hard her life had become.

"This is all Andy's fault! He was so self-centered! That's why my life is so miserable now. This is all my mama's fault. She treated her pit bull better than she treated me! It's not fair because I was such a good person to them. Nobody in this whole country understands me because I'm from Guam and I'm different! I should just go back to Guam. We're all about respect and honor back home—except for my mama and her dog. People here just don't get where I'm coming from. What do you think, Brenda? You see what I'm saying, don't you?" Sirena said forcefully.

Brenda told Sirena truthfully that she needed to change her thinking. "Stop attacking people. Take a look at yourself. Change your heart and change your mind," she stated bluntly. Sirena was insulted. After that day, she completely stopped talking to Brenda and bad-mouthed her to everyone she knew. "How dare she speak to me like that! Who does she think she is? She thinks she's better than everyone else. She's crazy! I'm so sick of her. I've put up with her nonsense for years! She'd better not say anything else, or I will tell her off. I don't need her lousy advice, and I don't ever need to deal with her again!" she said in a fit of rage.

It seemed so much easier to blame others than to examine her own conscience. Sirena thought that accusing other people would make her feel better, but she only felt frustrated. As several long and lonely months dragged by without anyone to hear her gripe, Sirena became tired of constantly feeling sorry for herself. "Help me, Jesus! I don't know what to do!" she cried.

In anguish, Sirena grabbed her pink rosary prayer beads and drove to church. She needed to clear her mind and find comfort, so the sanctuary of the church seemed like the best place in town. Very quietly, she stepped inside the large church building and sat in the corner. "Maybe I'm just meant to live a life of misery, loneliness, and inner chaos," she grumbled in desolation. As she sat there, a big part of her felt as if God had stopped listening to her prayers long ago.

Brenda gave Sirena some heartfelt advice.   *"Oh no you didn't!"* **Sirena exclaimed.**

When she looked up and stared at the cross, though, all she could think of was God's love and commitment. She suddenly found herself asking God to show her the way to love. "Teach me, Lord. Help me to know and understand you," she pleaded. Running away was the only thing Sirena knew about these days. She had run from relationships, she had run from love, and she had run from herself. "I'm sick of running," she said under her breath.

In the silence of the sanctuary, Sirena remembered something that her spiritually over-zealous neighbor had said to her recently. "God is a loving Father who gave us his only Son to bring us back to him. Go back to God! Return to our Father!" Her neighbor had sensed that she needed to hear some uplifting words, but she had refused to hear about God that day. Sarcastically, she had replied: "What does the word *Father* really mean? I've never had a Father, and I am just *fine* without one."

Right now, though, she did not feel fine at all. She did not want to deny God's love anymore. Her heart was aching so badly. She was tired of lying to herself and pretending to be strong on her own. She just wanted to pour out her whole heart to him—and she had nothing to hide because he already knew her heart better than anyone. Tears dripped onto her bright red tube top. Sirena was tired of holding on to her pride. She had thought that anger and pride made her stronger, but it only made her feel like a prisoner. She wouldn't be a slave to it anymore.

Sirena went to confession that evening and let out everything she had been holding inside. "I've been too proud to admit all the things I've done wrong. I stopped listening to the Lord," she said as she wept in sorrow. "I've been bitter, spiteful, and hateful. I've hurt so many people, including myself." The priest said a prayer about God's mercy and forgive-ness, and in the name of the Father, the Son, and the Holy Spirit, she was absolved of her sins. Before she left, he said: "That is not who you truly are. Go forth as a child of God."

Sirena felt peace inside. She was so happy that she could be reconciled to the Lord and his holy Church, which Christ himself had given his authority to heal and pardon. She wanted to give thanks to God, hear his Word, and receive Holy Communion, the conse-crated bread and wine, which was a *sacrament (a sacred sign)* of love, unity, and devo-tion, so she attended Mass that evening. During the Lord's Supper, a celebration of the *Eucharist*, which means *thanksgiving*, her heart was filled with gratitude, hope, and joy as she watched the simple bread and wine become something divine. It was Jesus, the Bread of Life, truly present before her in this spiritual food and drink. Through the words of Christ spoken by the priest, and the power of the Holy Spirit, the bread was now his Body and the wine was now his Blood. She offered her whole life to him, uniting herself to him as she hum-bly prayed in his holy presence. She held out her hands to receive Holy Communion and consumed his sacred Body and Blood, knowing he was truly present within her, nourishing her soul.

Tears of joy streamed down her face as she drove home in the darkness of the night. Her black mascara smudged her cheeks, but she did not care how she looked. She did not need ten perfect coats of mascara just to feel loved. In her heart, she knew that God had never given up on her or stopped listening to her prayers. He had been waiting for her to come back to him with all her heart. He loved her endlessly. Jesus, the Lamb of God, had sacrificed his very life by dying on the cross so that sins could be forgiven. The night before he died, during the breaking of the bread with his disciples, he freely offered his Body, his Blood, his Soul, and the very Divine Person that he is. He gave thanks and broke the bread, saying: "This is my body, which will be given for you; do this in memory of me" and "This cup is the new covenant in my blood, which will be shed for you." The Body, Blood, Soul and Divinity of Christ was the most precious gift that anyone could receive.

Christ has Died, Christ is Risen, Christ Will Come Again!

Sirena cried tears of joy.

Sirena knew that receiving this precious gift of Jesus' Body, Blood, Soul and Divinity in the Eucharist would give her the strength to go out into this world with all its beauty, splendor, and allurement, its confusion, suffering, and heartache, and see past her own selfish desires. His strength would allow her to joyfully serve those around her so they too could know the undying love of our Lord Jesus Christ, the living God who has risen from the dead. She knew that above all, the Lord wanted his children to gather together as one family, one bread, one body, to be united to him and partake of his divine life so they could be a visible sign on this earth of his eternal love for everyone. His love was a reality. Jesus was—and always would be—the way, the truth, and the life.

Being in such close communion with the Lord and reaching out to receive his forgiveness made Sirena realize that she needed to forgive others just as she had been forgiven. She loved to obsess over all the bad things she felt people had done to her, but dwelling on these thoughts only made her feel like she was going in circles. She had spent many years seeking things that never satisfied her soul. She had hungered and thirsted for people to agree with her negative outlook on life. She had yearned to have someone take her side whenever she put other people down. She had craved the attention of guys on the Internet who did not even care about her. Whenever the temptation to be self-centered came her way, she carelessly surrendered to it, and her interior greed and wrath quickly became a dreadful burden.

Each time that she gave up her willful, defiant ways for the joy of the Lord, though, she felt liberated. "You're the one I need, Lord! Thank you, Father, for your love!" she said joyfully. The truth had set her free. She did not have to live in misery anymore. Her spirit was coming back to life. She did not have to wait until she died to experience God's love as she had wrongly told herself so many times before. She felt the Lord's restoring power right at that moment. She started listening attentively during Mass on Sunday and began reading the Catechism (teachings) of the Catholic Church, as well as online Catholic Daily Meditations based on the Daily Mass Readings, although delving deeper into bible verses seemed practically foreign to her at first.

When she finally opened her heart to it, her mind was renewed, and she discovered she was more familiar with the scriptures than she had thought. She had been blessed growing up in the Church as a child, hearing all of the Gospels, but she had taken this for granted, along with the *graces*, the *gifts of God* given to her through the *sacraments, outward signs of inward grace* like Baptism, which Christ had instituted. She had been like an ungrateful child rejecting a Christmas present, treating it like garbage. But now, coming home to Jesus in his Church and remembering him at the feast set before her was the best present ever. She wanted to embrace Jesus, the Living Word of God, responding to his gift of faith and drawing close to him through prayer, Church teachings, by keeping her baptismal promises, frequently receiving the sacraments of Reconciliation and Holy Communion, celebrating and participating in the Mass, reaching out to those in need and loving even her enemies, and by cherishing both Sacred Tradition and Sacred Scripture. She could see the love of Jesus flowing through each one of these instruments of grace, leading her to the shining light of his salvation.

Jesus was her good shepherd beside her always. He was the way home to eternal life with the Father. "He calls his own sheep by name and leads them out," she read out loud, taking total comfort in the words of scripture. She did not have to feel lost, alone, confused, and afraid, wondering who she really was inside. God had not given her a spirit of cowardice, but of power, love, and self-control. She could see herself clearly now. She belonged to the Lord. She was part of the Body of Christ, and she was a daughter of God. Her doubts and fears were being replaced with the promises of God our Father in heaven. *This is what it means to have a loving Father*, Sirena thought. *He wants to show me a greater depth of love than I could ever dream of having.*

As she delved into the bible, it struck her that being kind and loving to people did not mean talking in a silky sweet voice. Flattery and superficial compliments always boosted her self-esteem, but flattery could be deceiving. Sirena thrived on being told how cute and charming she was, even when she was at her worst behavior. She realized that love was not a romantic soap opera or all about beautiful, fanciful words. Sometimes it involved being warned that you were heading for trouble.

God had been speaking to Sirena's heart for a long time, urging her to change, but in the past, she had not listened to the promptings of his Spirit. This time, however, she needed to seek his counsel. She needed him to advise and correct her so she could deal with her damaged relationships. She never really offered the best of her heart to anyone these days, and it was a pretty shallow existence. Deep down, she longed for true friendship. Sirena really missed her friend Brenda, although she had *dissed* her months ago. She knew that Brenda genuinely cared about her, so she set aside her pride and called her on the phone to apologize. "I'm really sorry, Brenda," Sirena said. "You don't have to apologize to me, Sirena, but don't pretend as if you don't have a problem. You disappeared for such a long time," Brenda responded.

Discussing problems frustrated and frightened Sirena, but she was committed to overcoming her fears with the help of God's grace. "Brenda, I have tried to be nice and polite, even when you were getting on my case. I was avoiding you because I didn't want to argue. You were acting so upset," she said. Brenda grimaced and replied: "Don't assume what other people are feeling. You were the only one who was upset. Pretending not to be mad does not make you a saint. Acting *nice and polite* is so meaningless when it's obvious that you're mad. Putting people down and insulting them does not work either. You have to fight for what is right with wisdom and love. You have it within yourself to do this, so just get past your bad feelings, and don't wait so long to forgive or say sorry. Treat people as if you actually care. You can't control others, and you can't force me to back you up every time you're annoyed with someone. Don't expect anyone to feel miserable just because you feel miserable. Quit burning bridges and learn to work things out with people."

Sirena tried not to roll her eyes as Brenda continued to say: "You think that it's the end of the world if you argue and face conflict, but you'll never work anything out with anyone—not with me, your mama, Andy, or anyone else—unless you talk things out. Don't give up so soon and walk away or be afraid to stand up for what's right in the eyes of God. If something is bugging you, get to the point and explain how you feel, instead of only hinting at it. Just say what you mean with truth and mercy in your heart. Share your honest emotions, but let go of your hatred and move forward with love. Keep giving your heart to the Lord. Keep picking up your cross every day and following him. Keep holding on to your faith. Only then can you remain at peace. It's a lifelong process to hold on to the peace that only God can give, but his love is worth every single second of it.

"I've learned to trust Jesus to help me through problems with my husband, children, and friends. I unite my sufferings to his cross, Sirena, because he turns suffering into an act of love. Cast aside your selfishness. Prayerfully unite your problems and sufferings to our Lord so he can turn them into a sacrifice of love that brings you closer to him and lets his grace fill your soul and the souls of others. Jesus had no sins, but he willingly suffered so much for us out of love when he laid down his life and was crucified, so he understands all our troubles, emotions, wounds, and pains. He even suffers with us now when we're hurting because we're members of his body. He knows everything we go through. Everyone has problems, and everyone has faults—including me—so don't think that you're the only one. We all need to pray for each other and encourage each other on this journey of life. Turn to the Lord for help and strength so you can face your issues with people. Be honest with him about what's going on inside of you. Be honest with yourself, and be honest with others. You're only hurting yourself, girl," Brenda explained.

**Brenda encouraged Sirena
to work things out with people.**

It was time to get real. Sirena knew everything Brenda had said was true, yet she found herself feeling incredibly mad at her all over again. She hated confrontation and melodrama though. Articulating her own feelings and sensitively addressing other people's feelings was not her specialty. She cringed whenever Brenda told her she was selfish and controlling, and she felt guilty telling Brenda that she was offensive at times, too. Sirena heaved a big sigh and finally said: "I've been so irritated with you for so many years about so many things you've said. You always tell me what I'm doing wrong as if you're my mother!" Sirena went on and on, listing all her grievances from the past few years.

"Sirena, I couldn't tell you everything was great when your whole mind-set was going down the tubes. It was more important to speak the ugly truth than to tell you a pretty lie. I am not your mother, but you keep thinking like a child and a victim. Start being the supportive friend that you want others to be to you," Brenda said.

"I'm glad that we're talking now, Sirena, but we'll keep having problems if you can't even acknowledge my point of view. Whenever you ask for my opinion, you get mad when I tell you how I feel. Am I supposed to see things your way only?" Brenda asked. Sirena always expected Brenda to understand her feelings perfectly, but she never bothered to consider Brenda's feelings. Sirena made a sincere effort to listen to what Brenda was telling her this time.

"I know you have a hard time speaking up, but you shouldn't let so many issues pile up like a trash heap. Ask the Lord to help you understand why you have this problem. You should have told me you were angry way back then, Sirena. Why do you keep so much junk inside for so many days, months, and years? You can't blame me for that because that was your decision, not mine. Take ownership of it and hold yourself accountable."

Sirena took a deep breath and replied: "I wish I had said something earlier, Brenda! That was my mistake. I was very mad at you—and I was very mad at myself for not speaking up—but those days are behind me now. I'm not anybody's victim, and I'm through with living in strife! I know that I need to make some changes, and I am working on it."

Sirena felt incredibly relieved after spitting out those words. Holding on to animosity was utterly exhausting. It was so much easier to have a candid conversation than to cling silently to her aggravation. After all, true friends cared about each other's feelings. She did not have to let resentment brew putridly like a cesspool in her heart any longer. "Thanks for talking to me, Brenda. I truly appreciate your friendship. Now I really have to go and make another phone call."

Sirena wanted to apologize to her mama most of all. That afternoon, she picked up the phone and dialed 6-7-1, Mama Manuela's Guam area code, to tell her she was sorry for hurting her so many times. Mama Manuela was quick to forgive her because she thought of Sirena as her 30-year-old baby, but part of her could not understand anything Sirena was saying. *Why was Sirena talking about asking God to help her work through her angry, bitter feelings so she could communicate better with people?* Mama Manuela simply could not relate to that.

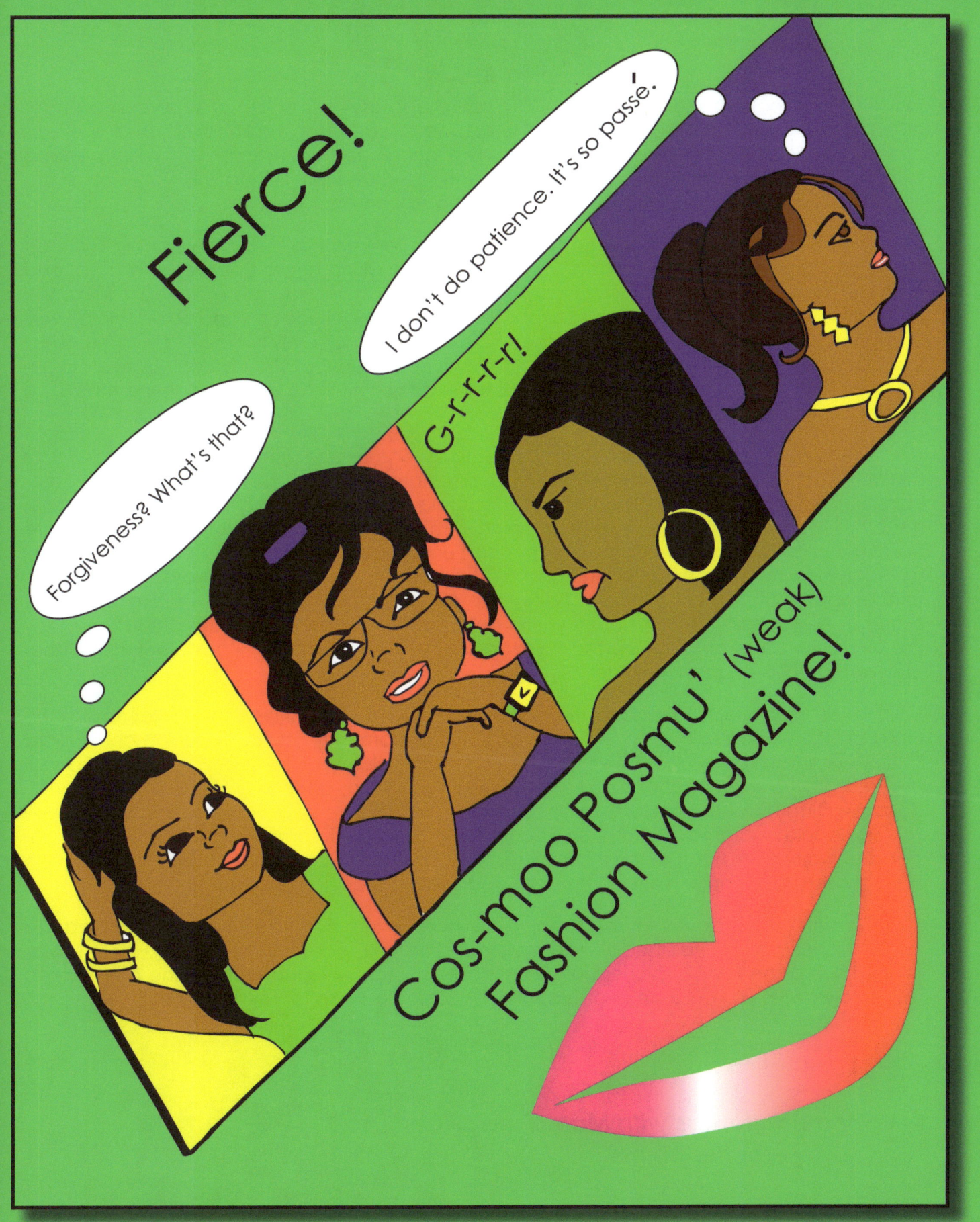

Mama Manuela used the good old passive-aggressive method of suppressing anger until she exploded. She taunted people with rude remarks and brash jokes when she was upset, instead of simply expressing what was bothering her. If anyone asked, "What's wrong with you, Manuela?" she would vehemently reply: "Something is wrong with you! You're too sensitive! I was just teasing because you're so *proud* and *banidosu*!"

She held an unspoken grudge against people for years, but she wore a big smile on her face in front of them. She blamed everybody for making her so unbelievably mad, and then she ran away and felt sorry for herself like a pouting child. She truly believed this was the most virtuous way to handle her frustration. She assured herself that no one could tell she was harboring ill will toward a single soul. "I like to be peaceful, *nai*. Only hypocrites like to argue," she would say, ironically. All her loved ones knew, however, that she had to win every argument as if it were a competition. They could tell exactly when she was in a fighting mood, no matter how dazzling her smile looked.

Sirena laughed when she thought about this. She realized she had learned many of her bad habits from Mama Manuela, but she also knew that Mama was nurturing, devoted, incredibly loving, and just plain funny. Sirena could picture her standing on the porch with her pit bull, chewing *betel nut*, and gossiping with her neighbors. She loved Mama despite her faults and knew that she had a tender heart underneath her cranky exterior. She remembered that Mama was the one who had first taught her how much she was loved by Jesus so that she would always be able to find her way back home to him whenever she went astray. The graceful, gentle woman within her mother's soul reminded her of Mother Mary, the Blessed Mother of God. Sirena told Mama that she was eternally grateful for all of her love before their phone call ended.

It was up to Sirena to cling to Jesus now, holding on tightly to his hand while moving forward as a grown up, allowing him to continually transform her interior life so she could grow in holiness and become more like him. She was not a helpless child. She was taking personal responsibility for all her actions. She was answering to God, after all. Her spirit no longer felt dead, waiting for people to love her or apologize to her. She could be the one to give love first. She could ask for forgiveness. She could tell loved ones if something was the matter, instead of waiting for them to read her mind. She could focus on someone else's needs for a change, serving people in her community and sharing the light of Christ.

God's love was molding and shaping her heart every day, showing her which road to travel. Sometimes life was filled with turmoil, but God kept carrying her through the fire. She offered him all her gratitude, her questions, her fears, sorrows, and worries. She often asked him, "How do I give your love to others, and what do you wish for my life, Lord?"

You don't mess with Mama — or her pit bull.

Sirena stopped becoming engrossed in her emotions, which changed every two seconds.

Happy   Sad   Bored

Her spirit was strong and steady deep within.

Another year flew by, and God definitely had big plans for Sirena, including things she could not envision yet. It was painful to admit, but Sirena still loved Andy. She longed for the day they could be together again, but she had almost given up all hope of reuniting with him. So much time had passed since going their separate ways. She prayed confidently that the Lord would heal her broken heart, even when tears filled her eyes.

In the past year, Andy and Sirena had barely spoken. Andy missed Sirena terribly, but he was too macho to admit it, even to himself. During the few times he had called her on the phone to make sure she had not gone off and married someone else, there was a wall of angst between them. Andy needed to know if she could give him another chance. He could not stop thinking about her anymore, but he was too proud to call her this time. He decided he would find out through her friend, Brenda, instead. If he called Brenda on the telephone, perhaps she would be willing to tell him all about Sirena's life.

"I can't speak for Sirena, Andy. Ask her yourself. You are so transparent. You still have feelings for her, so hurry up and talk to her," Brenda advised him.

It took over a month, but Andy finally stopped being so uptight and gathered the courage to contact Sirena. "Why are you calling me, Andy?" Sirena whispered breathlessly, feeling excited but apprehensive when she heard Andy's voice on the line. "Oh, I just wanted to talk to you and see how you're doing, Seeray-nuh," Andy casually responded, trying not to give his emotions away. "Oh, is that so?" Sirena replied skeptically as Andy chuckled guiltily.

Andy started calling her every day, over the next few months, hoping she would agree to the plans he had for them. "We can find a way to be together soon, Seeray-nuh! Don't you think this is a good time?" he asked her.

"Andy, I don't want us to have a half-hearted relationship," Sirena immediately replied in a firm and straightforward manner. Broken promises, hostile communication, and an unwillingness to make a true commitment were not going to cut it this time. Sirena knew it was an all-or-nothing situation. They were going to have to give it everything they had if they wanted to make it work.

Andy's response to this came tumbling out all at once. "Seeray-nuh, I just want us to be together! I want to get married to you! Let's start making our plans! What do you think?"

"We have been saved, we are being saved, and we will be saved."

As Andy elaborated on his plans for their future, Sirena's mind flashed back to their college days. She thought about all the years that had passed. No matter how many times they broke up and gave up, they still held on to each other. She felt so mad at him sometimes, but she missed him so much. She wished they could live their whole lives together. They both had hurt each other in the past, but she wished they could start over again. Sirena wanted to build a better relationship with Andy. She wanted a marriage that was based on God's love—a marriage that was a sign of Christ's enduring love for his bride, the Church.

Could they be patient and kind, always persevering, protecting, and trusting each other? Could they forgive each other over and over again as Jesus wanted? Could they let God's great love come first in their lives and bind them together during conflict and hardship, cleaving to each other as husband and wife under the Lord's protective care? Was Andy ready to work with her like a grown up?

Sirena needed to know how Andy felt about these things because they had always argued like children. Before she could ask him, Andy announced suddenly: "Listen, Seeray-nuh, this is how we should get married. I know we have some problems with each other, but it is no big deal! We'll be all right somehow. So, this is the way I want to do things…and this is when I want to do things…and this is how we should plan things…"

Sirena chewed on her raggedy fingernail stubs. She was nervous but ready to tell Andy everything in her heart. "Andy, you are the only one for me. I want to marry you too, but our problems are a big deal. We need to learn to work our problems out together. Are we going to allow the Lord to guide us through conflict, instead of doing things our own selfish way like before? Can we work together, side-by-side? Will you help me pull the **carabao** cart—I mean, the **water buffalo** cart—and grow a garden of love for the Lord? I can't pull this cart alone. I'm ready for the hard work, as well as the harvest…are you?"

Andy listened as Sirena shared her heart with him. But why was she talking about *carabao carts and harvests*? He became scared that Sirena was rejecting him, so he grasped for words. "But, but why-y-y, Seeray-nuh? What are you talking about?" Andy cried out. "I'm ready to shape up, Andy, but you seriously need to shape up, too. We just need to grow up. I'm sure you would also like our relationship to improve, but that takes effort. It requires forgiveness, patience, and humility on both our parts. Don't you think we could benefit from discussing our concerns and listening to each other better? Think about it, okay? This is important for both of us," Sirena said, before they told each other goodbye. She felt so glad that she had addressed these vital matters. Still, she did not know how things would turn out.

She realized that she might lose him, but they would only hurt each other if they were not ready to work together as a couple. She understood that a marriage flourishes with God as its stronghold. She knew that it was a *vocation, a special call from God. Was God calling each of them to the married life? Were they both ready to respond to his call and rely on his grace to help them build a life together?* Sirena had contemplated marriage a great deal lately, praying, discerning, and learning about it. Andy seemed to be sure they were meant to be together. Still, she needed to be certain.

She knew that the sacrament of Matrimony involves a husband and wife *fully, freely, faithfully, and fruitfully* giving their lives to one another as a marvelous, gleaming sign that radiates Christ's loving presence in this world. Marriage was a living symbol of Christ's intimate bond with his bride, the Church. His redeeming love for his beloved bride, the Church, was the greatest love story of all time. He had called his beloved to be joined to him, united to him forever, to be brought back into his loving embrace, back into his heavenly home within his sacred heart. It was obvious that marriage was intense. It was more than a commitment. It was an everlasting, binding *covenant* from God—*a sacred family bond, a sacred oath or vow, a sacred sign, a sacred action, a sacred event—a sacrament.* She knew she could not take Holy Matrimony lightly.

Entering into marriage was a big decision. Sirena trusted God with her life, no matter what happened. She prayed thankfully to him for being so good to her. Her faith was strong that the Lord would help her and Andy through this tumultuous time, even if it meant letting each other go. *Were they ready to put their whole hearts into marriage? Was Andy prepared to dedicate his life to Sirena as an ever-loving husband? Was Sirena ready to entrust herself to his loving care?* A couple of days went by as Sirena and Andy took some time to think about it. Finally, Andy called again. His voice sounded shaky when he said hello. What could that mean? Sirena's heart pounded strongly in her chest. *What if Andy had completely changed his mind? What if he was only calling to say goodbye?* Sirena did not know what the future held. She only knew that she was determined to live a life of love. "I know all your dreams in life will come true, Andy," Sirena said with sincerity.

"I know yours will, too," Andy replied with urgency in his voice. "I want things to be different this time. I want it to be better, Seeray-nuh. You are my only love. We'll make our dreams come true together. I also want God to help us live a good life so we can share his goodness with everyone. I pray for us every day. I know marriage is serious. You don't have to pull the carabao cart alone! I will be right there for you. I will give you everything I am. I know I'm not very good at telling you how I feel, but I am ready for the hard work, Seeray-nuh...are you?" Andy asked. At the bottom of it all, Sirena knew Andy would sacrifice his own comfort just to make her feel safe and loved. Sirena was also ready to love, honor, and give Andy the respect that she knew he appreciated and longed to have from her. "Yes, I'm ready! That's all I've been hoping for, Andy. God wants the best life for us!" Sirena replied in jubilation. Deep within their spirits, they still loved each other. This time, Sirena and Andy meant every word they said. God had given them all the faith, hope, and love they needed. They knew he would continue renewing their hearts during this journey of a lifetime and beyond.

♥

God had given them a spirit of love.

Love is patient, love is kind. It is not jealous,

[love] is not pompous, it is not inflated,

it is not rude, it does not seek its own interests,

it is not quick-tempered, it does not brood over injury,

it does not rejoice over wrongdoing, but rejoices with the truth.

It bears all things, believes all things, hopes all things,

endures all things. Love never fails.

So faith, hope, love remain, these three;

but the greatest of these is love.

(1 Corinthians 13:4-8, 13)

Love is charity, cherishing God above all things.
It means loving your neighbor as yourself,
being generous of heart.

If you make your home inside of God's heart, he will make his home inside of yours.
Father, we are yours!

Fight for Love!

Let your loved one share his or her feelings.
Don't talk back! Stay focused!
Be patient and listen to what is being said.
Now it's your turn!
Take turns speaking.

You mean you actually want me to help pull that contraption?

A Labor of Love

Christ is the Answer.
Depend on Him.
Jesus, I Trust in You!

Communication Garden

Talking + Understanding = Love & Respect

You have made us for yourself, O Lord,
and our hearts are restless until they rest in you.
– *St. Augustine*

Holiness consists simply in doing God's will,
and being just what God wants us to be.
– *St. Thérèse of Liseux*

Love the LORD, your God, follow him in all his ways,
keep his commandments, hold fast to him, and serve him with
your whole heart and your whole self. *(Joshua 22:5)*

Jesus said, "I thirst."
(John 19:28)

He thirsts for the love of souls.

Come and quench the thirst of Jesus.
– *Inspired by Bl. Mother Teresa*

**Yet the world and its enticement are passing away.
But whoever does the will of God remains forever.** *(1 John 2:17)*
Love One Another!

About the Author

Maris Lobdell D'souza (*familian Borja*, which means *of the Borja family*) grew up in the village of Agat, by the sea, on the island of Guam. As a child, she spent many years covertly cartooning in the back of the classroom at Agat Elementary School, Piti Middle School, and Oceanview High School, instead of "using her time wisely" like her Filipino teachers demanded every day. Growing up, she was an avid reader of the Pacific Daily News, which inspired her to receive a journalism degree from the University of Central Oklahoma.

Today, she writes short stories as a hobby. She also loves computer graphic design, as well as craft making. Currently, she resides in Texas with her husband and children. She has not forgotten the loving people from her island, who pray together and support each other, with the love of Christ.

Fill my cup Lord, I lift it up, Lord!
Come and quench this thirsting of my soul.
Bread of heaven, feed me till I want no more.
Fill my cup, fill it up and make me whole!

– R. Blanchard

www.ingramcontent.com/pod-product-compliance
Lightning Source LLC
Chambersburg PA
CBHW041003170626
46815CB00002B/145